ALYSSA

BUNNIES
and Their Sports

By Nancy Carlson

Viking Kestrel

Dedicated to children everywhere
who get out and exercise

VIKING KESTREL

Viking Penguin Inc., 40 West 23rd Street, New York, New York 10010, U.S.A.
Penguin Books Ltd, Harmondsworth, Middlesex, England
Penguin Books Australia Ltd, Ringwood, Victoria, Australia
Penguin Books Canada Limited, 2801 John Street, Markham, Ontario, Canada L3R 1B4
Penguin Books (N.Z.) Ltd, 182–190 Wairau Road, Auckland 10, New Zealand

Copyright © Nancy Carlson, 1987
All rights reserved
First published in 1987 by Viking Penguin Inc.
Published simultaneously in Canada
Printed in Japan by Dai Nippon Printing Co. Ltd.
Set in Bookman Light
1   2   3   4   5   90   89   88   87   86

Library of Congress Cataloging in Publication Data
Carlson, Nancy L.   Bunnies and their sports.
Summary: Reveals bunnies involved in jogging,
swimming, and exercising at the gym.
1. Sports—Juvenile literature.   [1. Rabbits—Wit and
humor.   2. Physical fitness—Wit and humor]   I. Title.
GV707.C35   1987   796   86-1337   ISBN 0-670-81109-2

Every morning when bunnies wake up from a good night's rest…

they brush their teeth, eat their breakfast,

and warm up.

Then it's time for bunnies and their sports!!!

Some bunnies like to jog…

others like to hike.

There are swimmer bunnies,

and bunnies who do swan dives.

Competitive bunnies like to play softball,

or touch football.

There are waterskiing bunnies,

and there are snow bunnies.

Sometimes many bunnies gather together

for a game of volleyball....

Brave bunnies go surfing,

or climb high mountains.

There are bunnies who go to gyms…

to lift weights,

...play basketball,

or do aerobics.

There are bunnies who roller-skate,

and bunnies who ice-skate.

Some bunnies like to exercise quietly by doing yoga,

or scuba diving deep underwater.

Some bunnies exercise outdoors, playing soccer, biking,

or playing tennis!!

Different bunnies like

different sports…

*but all bunnies do sports because
they make them feel good!!!*